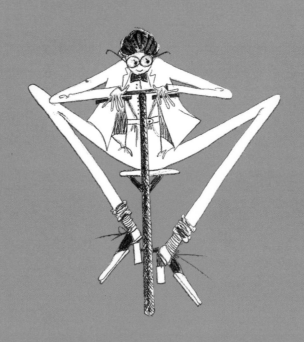

Mr. Munson's It

Written by Nancy Nolan, M.A.   Illustrated by Kathryn Scadden, B.F.A., M.A.

BEAVER'S
POND
PRESS

ISBN 978-1-59298-981-2

Library of Congress Catalog Number: 2013908920

Printed in the United States of America

First Printing: 2013

16 15 14 13   4 3 2 1

Words by Nancy Nolan
Illustrations by Kathryn Scadden
Edited by Lily Coyle
Book design by Sara Weingartner

BEAVER'S
POND
PRESS

Beaver's Pond Press, Inc.
7108 Ohms Lane
Edina, MN 55439-2129
(952) 829-8818
www.BeaversPondPress.com

www.mrmunsonsitvice.com

To Skip and David

and

Brad, Connell, Melissa, Margaret,
Elizabeth, Ned, and Xavi

...and of course, to Sara

There's Ellie, Ellie Lou Butler.
She's the last one getting off the bus.
Ellie is in Ms. Gallagher's class at Pickle
Pond Elementary School.

There, over there by the bike rack is Mr. Munson.
He's the guidance counselor at Pickle Pond.

Pickle Pond Elementary School

1

Every morning when Ellie walks into school, she sees Mr. Munson. He stands at the front door and greets everyone in a friendly way.

"Hello, Margaret and Elizabeth."
"Hello, Mr. Munson."

"Totally terrific Tuesday, Ned."
"Totally terrific Tuesday, Mr. Munson."

"Good morning, Ellie."
"Good morning, Mr. Munson."

Recess is that time of day
when all the children have
fun on the playground with
their friends. All the children,
that is, except Ellie.

4

Ellie walks around the
playground looking sad.
No one asks her to play.
No one looks friendly.
No one even notices her.

5

Mr. Munson is not in his office. So, Ellie leaves him a note on his desk.

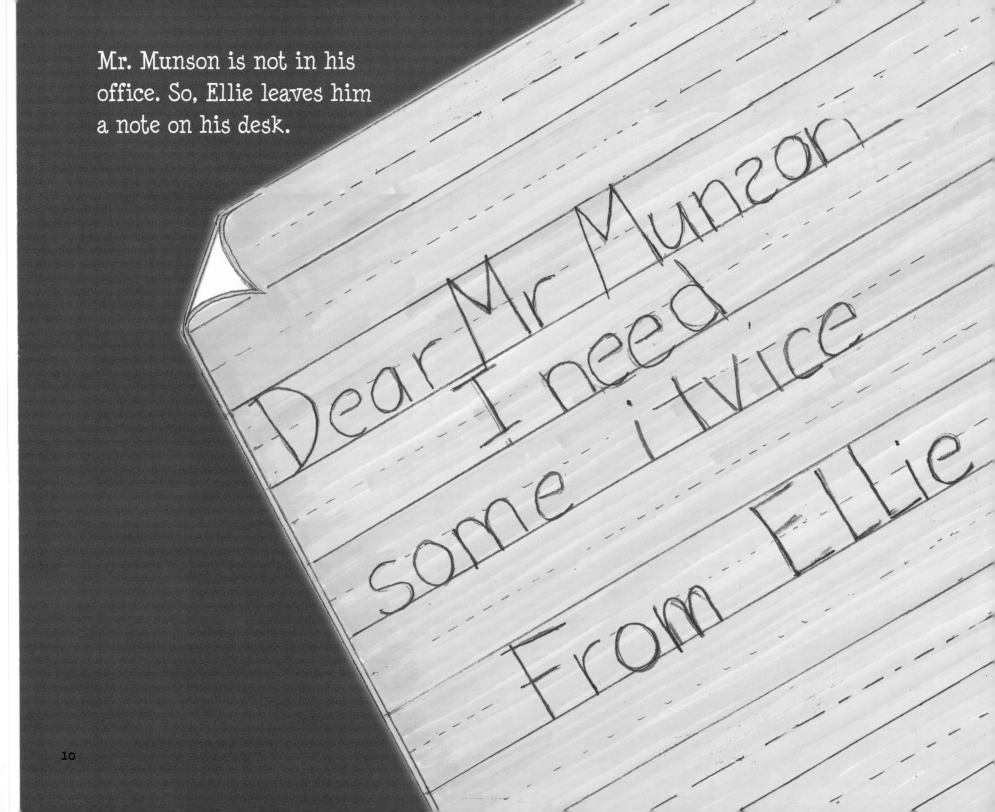

Mr. Munson invites Ellie into his office. She's very quiet. She's not sure what to say. This is hard.

"How can I help you, Ellie?" says Mr. Munson. "Your note says that you need some itvice."

"I'm having a problem with friends," says Ellie. "Kids don't want to play with me. They're not very nice to me, and I don't think they like me. Can you help me, Mr. Munson?"

"There's a secret to friendship, Ellie," says Mr. Munson. "It's kind of easy, and it's kind of hard. To have friends, first, you have to be the kind of person that others like to be around."

"Huh?" says Ellie. "I don't understand."

"Well, that means you smile at others. You ask kids questions about themselves. You share. You take turns. You offer to help. You ask others to join you in a game," says Mr. Munson.

"What if I'm not good at being a friend, Mr. Munson? What if I just can't make friends?"

Ellie tries Mr. Munson's 'itvice.' At recess that day, she smiles at some kids, and they all smile back at her.

When she sees those smiles, it feels okay to say, "hi" and introduce herself.
Ellie learns the names of many new kids.

Then, she decides to ask some kids a few questions about themselves.

"What did you think about the math test we took this morning?"

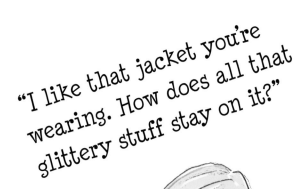

"I like that jacket you're wearing. How does all that glittery stuff stay on it?"

"What rope-jumping songs do
you know?"

"Are you playing four square?
What are the rules to this game?"

20

"What color do you get when you mix yellow and red?"

"Do you want to go down the slide

together?"

"You must be the new student. Hi, my name is Ellie. What's your name?"

Ellie has lots of fun at recess today. She even makes plans
to have lunch with some of these kids tomorrow.

It's hard work, but each day, it gets easier to talk to other kids. Each day, recess becomes more fun, and each day Ellie learns a little more about friendship. "That's what Mr. Munson means about taking it one step at a time," says Ellie.

After a few days of making friends, Ellie writes another
note to Mr. Munson. This is what it says:

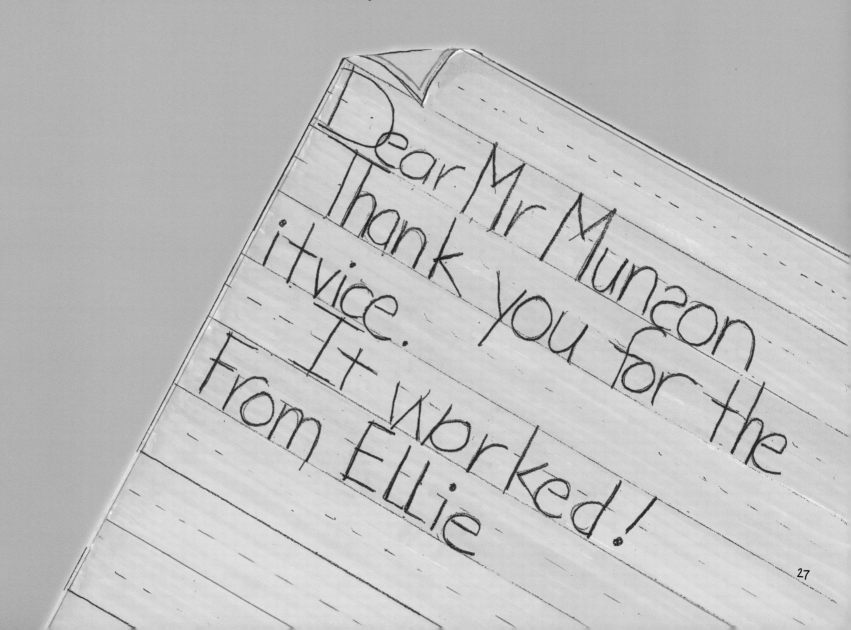

Dear Mr Munson
Thank you for the
itvice. It worked!
From Ellie

Mr. Munson's Friendship Advice:

1. Smile at others and say, "hi."
2. Ask their names; tell them your name.
3. Show an interest by asking questions.
4. Listen.
5. Share.
6. Be kind.
7. Take it one step at a time.
8. Be the friend you want to have.
9. Practice. Practice. Practice.

Here are some questions you could ask:

1. What is your name? Where do you live?
2. What games do you like to play?
3. How did our teacher make that science experiment work?
4. Why do you think we had a fire drill this morning?
5. What is your favorite book? Who is your favorite author?
6. What kind of pet do you have?
7. What are you going to do in the talent show next week?

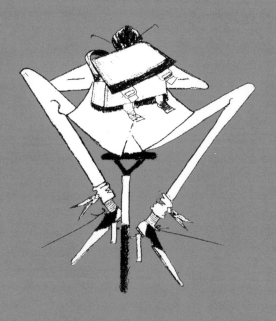

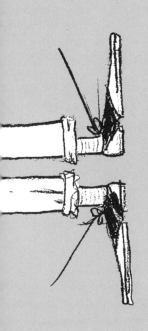